How the Whale got his Throat

Rudyard Kipling
Illustrated by Pauline Baynes

PETER BEDRICK BOOKS
NEW YORK

First American edition published in 1987 by Peter Bedrick Books 125 East
23 Street New York, NY 10010. Published by agreement with Macmillan
Children's Books, a division of Macmillan Publishers Ltd., London &
Basingstoke.

Library of Congress Cataloging-in-Publication Data
    Kipling, Rudyard, 1865–1936.
        How the whale got his throat.

        (A Just so story)
        Summary: Relates how a clever little fish and a mariner of
    "infinite-resource-and-sagacity" modify the whale's throat to keep
    him from devouring all the fish in the ocean.
        [1. Whales—Fiction.] I. Baynes, Pauline, ill. II. Title. III. Series:
    Kipling, Rudyard, 1865–1936. Just so stories.
    PZ7.K632Ho   1987   [E]   86-28854
    ISBN 0-87226-135-2 (lib. bdg.)

Printed in Hong Kong
Reinforced binding

IN the sea, once upon a time, O my Best Beloved, there was a Whale, and he ate fishes. He ate the starfish and the garfish, and the crab and the dab, and the plaice and the dace, and the skate and his mate, and the mackereel and the pickereel, and the really truly twirly-whirly eel. All the fishes he could find in all the sea he ate with his mouth—so! Till at last

there was only one small fish left in all the sea, and he was a small 'Stute Fish, and he swam a little behind the Whale's right ear, so as to be out of harm's way. Then

the Whale stood up on his tail and said, 'I'm hungry.'
And the small 'Stute Fish said in a small 'stute voice,
'Noble and generous Cetacean, have you ever tasted
Man?'

'No,' said the Whale. 'What is it like?'

'Nice,' said the small 'Stute Fish. 'Nice but nubbly.'

'Then fetch me some,' said the Whale, and he made
the sea froth up with his tail.

'One at a time is enough,' said the 'Stute Fish. 'If you
swim to latitude Fifty North, longitude Forty West (that
is Magic), you will find, sitting *on* a raft,*in* the middle of
the sea, with nothing on but a pair of blue canvas
breeches, a pair of suspenders (you must *not* forget the
suspenders, Best Beloved), and a jack-knife, one
shipwrecked Mariner, who, it is only fair to tell you, is a
man of infinite-resource-and-sagacity.'

So the Whale swam and swam to latitude Fifty North,

longitude Forty West, as fast as he could swim, and *on* a

raft, *in* the middle of the sea, *with* nothing to wear except a pair of blue canvas breeches, a pair of suspenders (you must particularly remember the suspenders, Best Beloved), *and* a jack-knife, he found one single, solitary

shipwrecked Mariner, trailing his toes in the water. (He had his Mummy's leave to paddle, or else he would never have done it, because he was a man of infinite-resource-and-sagacity.)

Then the Whale opened his mouth back and back and
back till it nearly touched his tail, and he swallowed the
shipwrecked Mariner, and the raft he was sitting on,
and his blue canvas breeches, and the suspenders
(which you *must* not forget), *and* the jack-knife. He
swallowed them all down into his warm, dark, inside
cupboards, and then he smacked his lips—so, and
turned round three times on his tail.

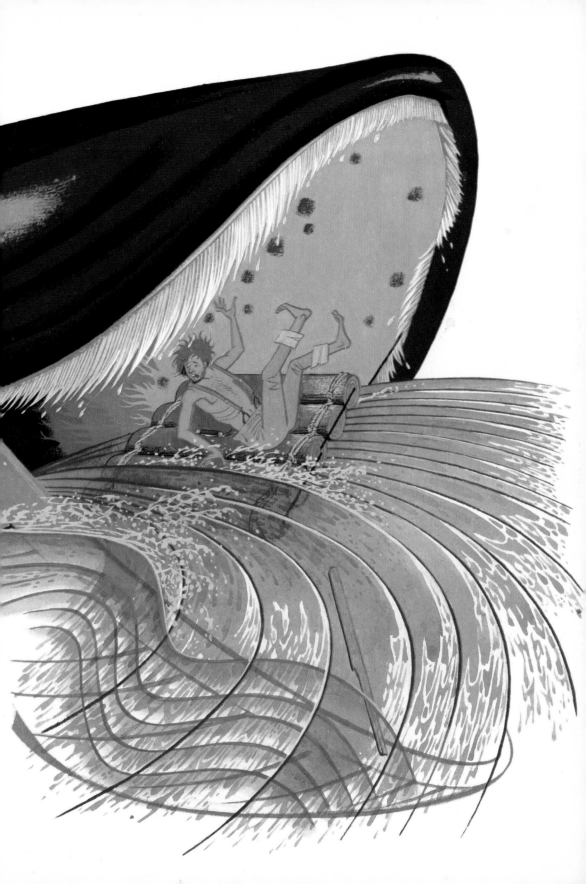

But as soon as the Mariner, who was a man of infinite-resource-and-sagacity, found himself truly inside the Whale's warm, dark, inside cupboards, he stumped and he jumped and he thumped and he

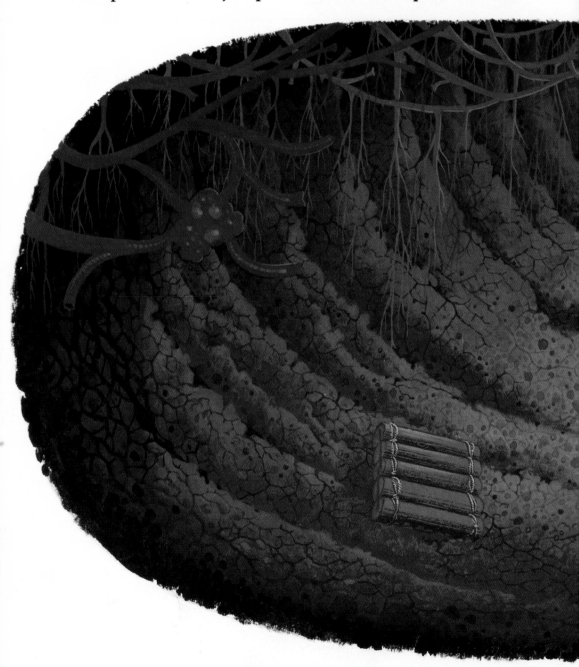

bumped, and he pranced and he danced, and he banged and he clanged, and he hit and he bit, and he leaped and creeped, and he prowled and he howled, and he

hopped and he dropped, and he cried and he sighed,

and he crawled

and he bawled,

and he stepped

and he lepped,

and he danced hornpipes where he shouldn't,
and the Whale felt most unhappy indeed. (*Have* you
forgotten the suspenders?)

So he said to the 'Stute Fish, 'This man is very nubbly, and besides he is making me hiccough. What shall I do?'

'Tell him to come out,' said the 'Stute Fish.

So the Whale called down his own throat to the shipwrecked Mariner, 'Come out and behave yourself. I've got the hiccoughs.'

'Nay, nay!' said the Mariner. 'Not so, but far otherwise. Take me to my natal-shore and the white-cliffs-of-Albion, and I'll think about it.' And he began to dance more than ever.

'You had better take him home,' said the 'Stute Fish to the Whale. 'I ought to have warned you that he is a man of infinite-resource-and-sagacity.'

So the Whale swam and swam and swam, with both flippers and his tail, as hard as he could for the hiccoughs; and at last he saw the Mariner's natal-shore and the white-cliffs-of-Albion, and he rushed half-way

up the beach, and opened his mouth wide and wide and wide, and said, 'Change here for Winchester, Ashuelot, Nashua, Keene, and stations on the *Fitch*burg Road'; and just as he said 'Fitch' the Mariner walked out of his mouth. But while the Whale had been swimming, the

Mariner, who was indeed a person of infinite-resource-and-sagacity, had taken his jack-knife and cut up the raft into a little square grating all running criss-cross, and he had tied it firm with his suspenders (*now* you know why you were not to forget the suspenders!), and he dragged that grating good and tight into the Whale's throat, and there it stuck! Then he recited the following *Sloka*, which, as you have not heard it, I will now proceed to relate:—

> *'By means of a grating*
> *I have stopped your ating.'*

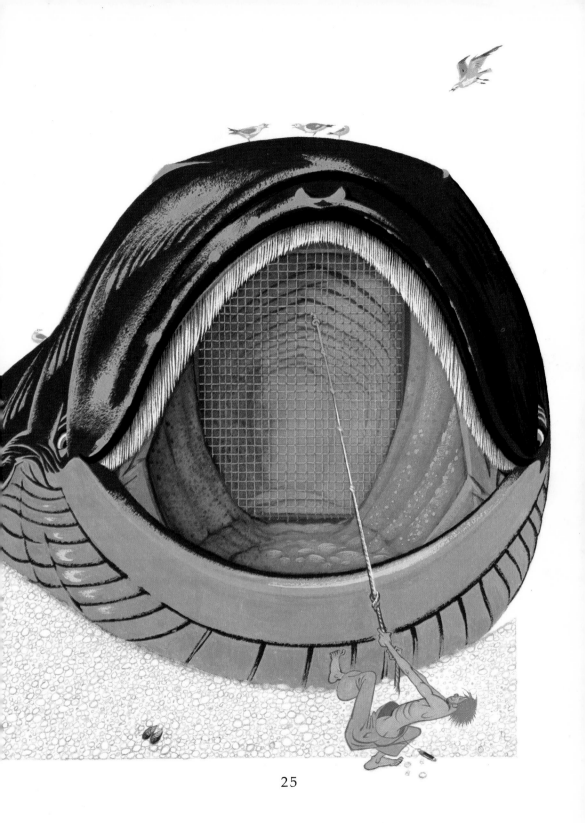

For the Mariner he was also an Hi-ber-ni-an. And he stepped out on the shingle, and went home to his Mother, who had given him leave to trail his toes in the water; and he married and lived happily ever afterward.

So did the Whale. But from that day on, the grating in his throat, which he could neither cough up nor swallow down, prevented him eating anything except very, very small fish; and that is the reason why whales nowadays never eat men or boys or little girls.

The small 'Stute Fish went and hid himself in the mud under the Door-sills of the Equator. He was afraid that the Whale might be angry with him.

The Sailor took the jack-knife home. He was wearing the blue canvas breeches when he walked out on the shingle. The suspenders were left behind, you see, to tie the grating with; and that is the end of *that* tale.

When the cabin port-holes are dark and green
    Because of the seas outside;
When the ship goes wop (with a wiggle between)
And the steward falls into the soup-tureen,
  And the trunks begin to slide;
When Nursery lies on the floor in a heap,
And Mummy tells you to let her sleep,
And you aren't waked or washed or dressed,
Why, then you will know (if you haven't guessed)
You're 'Fifty North and Forty West!'

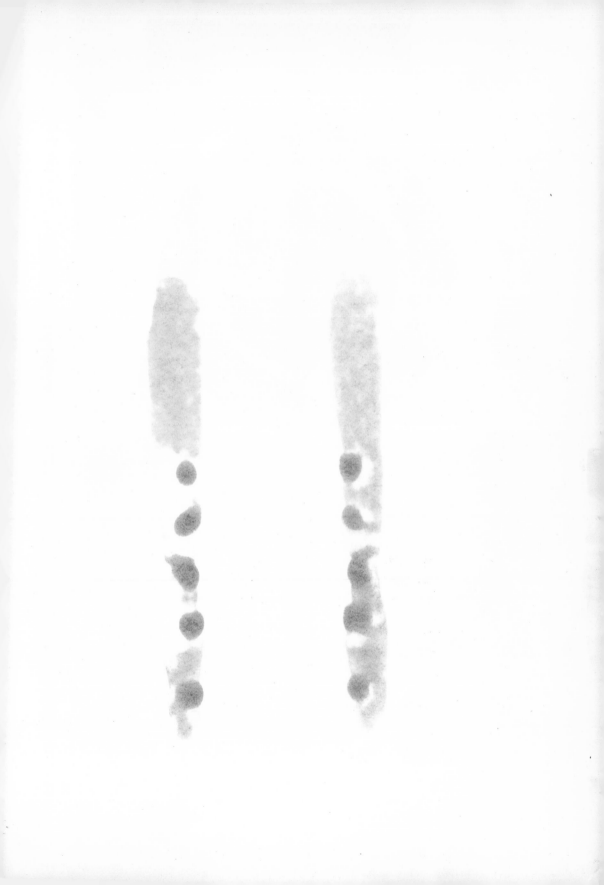

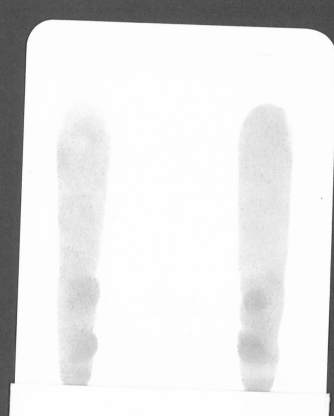